It's Mine!

First published in the United States 1988 by
Dial Books for Young Readers
A Division of NAL Penguin Inc.
2 Park Avenue
New York, New York 10016

Published in Great Britain by Hutchinson Children's Books
Printed in Italy
First Edition
O B E
1 3 5 7 9 10 8 6 4 2

Library of Congress Cataloging in Publication Data
de Lynam, Alicia Garcia. It's mine!
Summary: Two young children discover that although it's
difficult to share a favorite toy, it can be even more
fun to play with it together.
[1. Sharing—Fiction. 2. Play—Fiction.
3. Behavior—Fiction.] I. Title.
PZ7.D33955It 1988 [E] 87-24649
ISBN 0-8037-0509-3

Alicia Garcia de Lynam

It's Mine!

Dial Books for Young Readers

New York

Here you are, Teddy.

Where's Tiger?

It's mine!

Get off my toys!

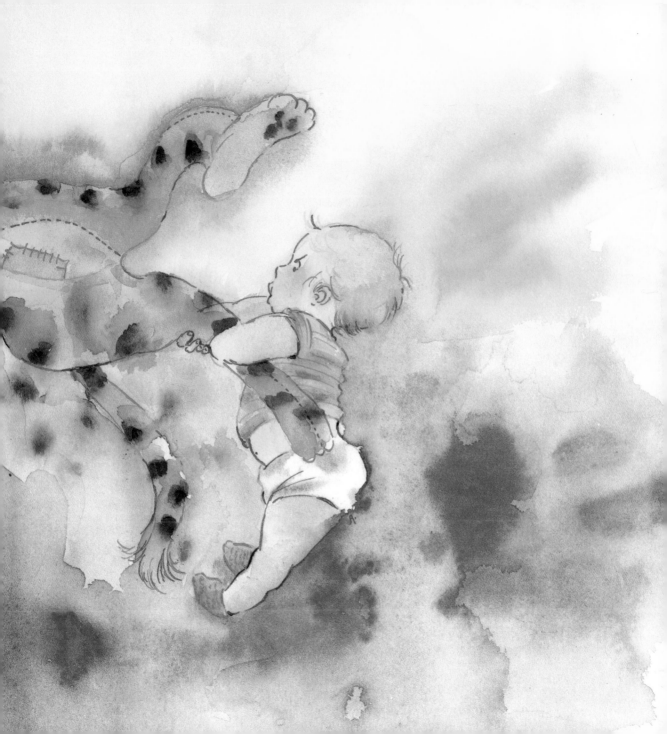

What's all this?

Play nicely,
then you can
have him back.

Don't cry, I'll get him.

Tiger's sorry.

You can play too, if you like.

I'll pour.

There's nothing like tea for two.

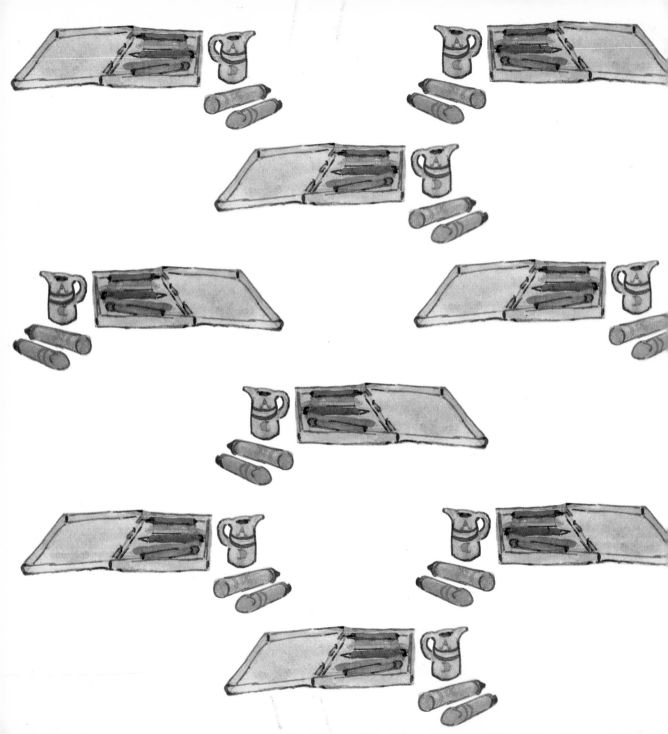